Weekly Reader Children's Book Club Presents

The After-Christmas Tree

Story by Linda Wagner Tyler

Pictures by Susan Davis

VIKING

This book is a presentation of Newfield Publications, Inc.
Newfield Publications offers book clubs for children
from preschool through high school. For further
information write: **Newfield Publications, Inc.,**
4343 Equity Drive, Columbus, Ohio 43228.

Published by arrangement with Viking Penguin,
a division of Penguin Books USA Inc.
Newfield Publications is a trademark
of Newfield Publications, Inc.
Weekly Reader is a federally registered trademark
of Weekly Reader Corporation.
Printed in the United States of America.

VIKING
Published by the Penguin Group
Viking Penguin, a division of Penguin Books USA Inc.
375 Hudson Street, New York, NY 10014 U.S.A.
Penguin Books Ltd, 27 Wrights Lane, London W8 5TZ, England
Penguin Books Australia Ltd, Ringwood, Victoria, Australia
Penguin Books Canada Ltd, 2801 John Street, Markham, Ontario, Canada L3R 1B4
Penguin Books (N.Z.) Ltd, 182-190 Wairau Road, Auckland 10, New Zealand
Penguin Books Ltd, Registered Offices: Harmondsworth, Middlesex, England

First published in 1990 by Viking Penguin, a division of Penguin Books USA Inc.
10 9 8 7 6 5 4 3 2
Text copyright © Linda Wagner Tyler, 1990
Illustrations copyright © Susan Davis, 1990
All rights reserved

Library of Congress Cataloging in Publication Data
Tyler, Linda Wagner: The after-Christmas tree
a winter story/by Linda Wagner Tyler: illustrated by Susan Davis. p. cm.
Summary: Family members take their Christmas tree into the backyard
and decorate it with edible trimmings for the wild birds and animals.
ISBN 0-670-83045-3 [1. Christmas trees—Fiction. 2. Christmas—Fiction.]
I. Davis, Susan, 1948- ill. II. Title.
PZ7.T94Af 1990 [E]—dc20 90-12166
Without limiting the rights under copyright reserved above, no part of this
publication may be reproduced, stored in or introduced into a retrieval
system, or transmitted, in any form or by any means (electronic, mechanical,
photocopying, recording or otherwise), without the prior written permission
of both the copyright owner and the above publisher of this book.

For my Mom and Dad,
thanks for my wonderful childhood years.
                                              —L.W.T.

For Sally, my twin, with love.
                              —S.D.

It was New Year's Day.

It was time to take down the Christmas tree.

I feel sad when Christmas is over.

We had fun making cards
and presents and
baking cookies.

Mom and Dad came to see our Christmas pageant.

We had a caroling party.

And we found the perfect
Christmas tree. It was so
tall we had to make extra
paper chains to fill it up.

"Why does such a great season have to end
so soon?" I asked Mom.
Mom said, "I have an idea to make it last longer.
Let's have a winter party."

THE
TYLERS

Please
come to our
After Christmas Party
Meet at the pond
on Saturday at 2 p.m.
Bring your ice skates.

We made invitations and sent them to our friends.

We spent the afternoon taking the decorations
and lights off our tree.

On Saturday we met at the pond.

The ice was like glass.

Dad was the leader and we made a snake.

When it was time to go home we gave everyone a bag and asked them to collect pinecones on the walk back.

Dad made popcorn and Mom said, "We are going to decorate our old Christmas tree with treats for the birds and wild animals so they will have enough food for the long winter ahead."

We gathered around the table and
covered the pinecones with peanut butter

and rolled them in birdseed.

We strung popcorn and berries.

Dad set the tree up in our yard.

We tied the pinecones to the branches with red ribbons.

Mom gave us nuts to spread around the base
of the tree.

When we were finished, our old tree didn't look so sad anymore. Then we went inside.

Mom and Dad passed out the hot chocolate
while we watched the party outside.

There were birds all over
the Christmas tree and the
squirrels were stuffing
their cheeks. Mom said,
"Our Christmas tree is
enjoying its second season
of giving."